Dragon Slayers' Academy™ 14

PIG LATIN— NOT JUST FOR PIGS!

By Kate McMullan

Illustrated by Bill Basso

GROSSET & DUNLAP

For all the Pig Latin scholars at Colorado
Academy in Denver, especially Gayle Breaux,
Suzy Hisky, and guinea Pig Latin expert,
Tina Rivera—K.M.

For James and Wei—B.B.

GROSSET & DUNLAP
Published by the Penguin Group
Penguin Group (USA) Inc., 375 Hudson Street, New York, New York 10014, U.S.A.
Penguin Group (Canada), 10 Alcorn Avenue, Toronto, Ontario, Canada M4V 3B2
(a division of Pearson Penguin Canada Inc.)
Penguin Books Ltd, 80 Strand, London WC2R 0RL, England
Penguin Ireland, 25 St Stephen's Green, Dublin 2, Ireland
(a division of Penguin Books Ltd)
Penguin Group (Australia), 250 Camberwell Road, Camberwell, Victoria 3124,
Australia (a division of Pearson Australia Group Pty Ltd)
Penguin Books India Pvt Ltd, 11 Community Centre, Panchsheel Park,
New Delhi - 110 017, India
Penguin Group (NZ), Cnr Airborne and Rosedale Roads, Albany, Auckland 1310,
New Zealand (a division of Pearson New Zealand Ltd)
Penguin Books (South Africa) (Pty) Ltd, 24 Sturdee Avenue, Rosebank,
Johannesburg 2196, South Africa

Penguin Books Ltd, Registered Offices:
80 Strand, London WC2R 0RL, England

Library of Congress Control Number: 2005001602

ISBN 978-0-448-43820-7   10 9 8 7 6

Chapter 1

Wiglaf lifted the bun on his sandwich. There was a pile of stringy brown glop underneath.

"Ikes-yay!" he cried, speaking Pig Latin.

"Yikes is right," muttered Angus. "What *is* it?"

"'Tis a moatweed sloppy joe," Erica answered. "Frypot's newest dish." She bit eagerly into her sandwich. Erica loved everything about DSA. Even the food.

"Uck-yay," Wiglaf muttered. "Yuck."

He had learned Pig Latin from his pet pig, Daisy. He now spoke it with ease.

A wizard had put a Speech Spell on Daisy. It was supposed to make her speak English.

But when Daisy opened her mouth, out came Pig Latin! And no wonder. The wizard was Zelnoc. He couldn't do even the most basic Wart-Be-Gone Spell or Sneeze-No-More Spell without messing it up. A Speech Spell was far beyond his powers.

"Ugh!" Angus pushed away his plate. "'Tis a good thing my mother sent me a giant goodie box this month."

Wiglaf watched longingly as Angus drew a Medieval Marshmallow Bar from his tunic pocket and took a bite. If only Angus liked to share! But alas—he did not.

"We had barley bran burgers for lunch at my old school," said Janice. "They tasted like dirt. But moatweed sloppy joes are worse."

"At Princess Prep," said Gwen, "we had princess-and-the-pea soup every day." She sighed. "I didn't like it much, but I'd trade my emerald tiara for a bowl of it right now!"

"Atten*tion!*" called Headmaster Mordred as

he strode into the DSA dining hall. His red velvet cape streamed out behind him. Thick dark hair sprang from his head. He wore shiny gold rings on all his fingers. And on both thumbs, too.

Wiglaf and the other students jumped up.

"At ease!" barked Mordred. "I have news!"

The dining hall grew so quiet that Wiglaf could hear the rats fighting over crumbs under the Class I table.

Mordred's violet eyes glowed with excitement. "I do not believe in wasting time with school vacations."

"That's not news, Uncle Mordred," said Angus. "We all know we've never had a single day off from school."

"At Dragon Whackers," said Janice, "we got a whole *week* off in the summer."

"Silence!" snapped the headmaster. "I have a treat for all you lads—and lasses!" Mordred smiled at the new girls. His gold tooth sparkled in the noonday light.

"Tomorrow, Saturday, and Sunday," he went on, "some very important people are coming to a meeting here at DSA."

"Is Sir Lancelot coming?" Erica asked eagerly. The famous knight was her hero. A tapestry of Sir Lancelot slaying a dragon hung on the wall above her cot in the Temporary Lasses' Dorm.

"No, the people who are coming are a—uh—teachers," Mordred said quickly. "Yes, that's it. Teachers. They are coming here so I can teach them how to be better teachers. So you lads and lasses get a three-day vacation. You get to go home."

"YAY! HOORAY!" cried the students.

They stomped and cheered. The noise sent the rats under the Class I table, dashing for their hole in the wall.

Home! Wiglaf had not been home in ever so long. He would see his mother, Molwena.

And his father, Fergus. And his twelve brothers. After eating Frypot's cooking at DSA, he was even looking forward to a big bowl of Molwena's cabbage soup.

"There is something fishy about this," Angus muttered as the cheering died down. "Uncle Mordred doesn't give a fig about better teachers."

"Go to your dorms and pack your bags," Mordred was saying. "Make your cots. Leave the dorm clean as a whistle." He reached for his hourglass and turned it upside down. "I want everyone out of here within the hour. Go on. Buh-bye!"

Wiglaf and the others raced from the dining hall, shouting, "Holiday! Holiday!"

The lads ran to their bunks. The lasses disappeared behind the burlap curtain that divided the Lads' Dorm from the Temporary Lasses' Dorm.

Erica reached under her cot and pulled out

the largest piece of her Lancelot-on-the-Go Luggage—a huge trunk with a handle and with wheels on the bottom. She began packing.

Wiglaf had no trunk. Or even a bag. So he spread his blanket out on his cot and began tossing his things onto it. His rusty sword, Surekill. His Lucky Rag.

"At home I shall ride my red pony," said Gwen, packing her tiara and fashion magazines.

"I shall go to the Toenail Fair," said Torblad. "And have my fortune told!"

"I shall go home to the palace and get the royal treatment," said Erica. She rolled up her Sir Lancelot tapestry and put it in her trunk. She packed her suit of Sir Lancelot armor. "What shall you do in Pinwick, Wiggie?"

"I shall..." Wiglaf stopped. He did not want to tell Erica that he would likely spend his holiday elbow-deep in greasy dishwater, scrubbing his mother's soup pot. Or picking cabbages. Or packed inside the hovel with his twelve smelly brothers, listening to their father's awful knock-knock jokes.

"I shall keep busy," he said at last.

"I shall sleep late." Angus grinned. "And eat cherry pie for breakfast."

"Angus," said Erica, "did you not tell me that your mother went to West Sheepdip?"

Angus's smile faded. "I forgot!" he cried. "Mother is visiting her cousin, Lady Flockbleet. Oh, woe! I cannot go home!"

"Come home with me to the palace, then," said Erica, buckling on her tool belt.

Angus wiped his nose. "Really?"

Erica nodded. "Chef Pierre can bake you a cherry pie for every meal."

"With whipping cream?" asked Angus.

"With whipping cream," said Erica.

"My parents are visiting my brother for Parents Weekend at Dragon Whackers," said Janice. "Is there room for me, too?"

"Sure!" said Erica. "The palace has 435 bedrooms. You can take your pick."

"Will you come home with me, too, Wiggie?" she said.

Wiglaf felt torn. He wanted to see his family. But here was a chance to stay at a real palace! A palace with a chef who baked cherry pies! A palace where someone else would wash the pots and pans. A palace where he might sleep in one of 435 bedrooms—all by himself!

Wiglaf was so very tempted! "Oh, but Daisy," he said, remembering. "I cannot leave her here."

"She can stay in the Royal Sty," said Erica.

Wiglaf smiled and bowed. "In that case, Daisy and I would love to come!"

Wiglaf's fingers trembled with excitement as he knotted his rope around his blanket. To think that he, a lowly Pinwick peasant, was going to the Royal Palace!

Chapter 2

"Waitest thou lads and lasses!" called Brother Dave. The chubby little monk came rushing across the castle yard toward the departing students. "Thou canst not journey with empty stomachs. Here!" He began handing out big chunks of his homemade peanut brittle from the basket he was carrying.

Wiglaf tucked a piece of the peanut candy into his pack. And a piece for Daisy, too.

"Thank you, Brother Dave," he said.

"Worrieth not about Worm," the monk whispered to Wiglaf, referring to the young dragon who sometimes hid out in the DSA library. "I shall looketh after him whilst thou art gone. Enjoyeth thy stay in Pinwick!"

"I am not going home, Brother Dave," Wiglaf said. "Erica has invited me to come home with her to the palace."

"Me too," said Janice.

"E-may ee-thray," said Daisy, which meant, "me three."

"Me four," Angus chimed in. "We shall eat cherry pie for breakfast, lunch, and supper. Oh, I cannot wait to get there!"

"Farewell, then, lads and lasses," said Brother Dave. "But remember, enjoyth thy journey. A journey canst bring wondrous surprises—and dangerous ones as well. Taketh care!"

"Oodbye-gay!" called Daisy.

"She's saying good-bye to you, Brother Dave," said Wiglaf.

"Fare thee well, Daisy," said the monk. "Farewell, all!"

Wiglaf waved. Then the travelers

walked through the gatehouse, over the DSA drawbridge, and turned north on Huntsman's Path.

Wiglaf stuck a long stick through the knot on his blanket so that he might carry it on his shoulder. His load was light, and he was glad.

Erica's trunk was not so light. Along with her Sir Lancelot tapestry and her Sir Lancelot armor, she had packed her Sir Lancelot dagger collection, a shoe from Sir Lancelot's steed, and her precious brick from Sir Lancelot's castle. She had tried to pack her Sir Lancelot first-aid kit and her Sir Lancelot beach towel. But alas! She could not squeeze in another item.

"How long does it take to reach the Royal Palace?" Wiglaf asked her.

"Many hours," Erica said, pulling the mammoth wheeled trunk behind her. "Unless we take the shortcut through the Dark Forest."

"Through the forest?" said Wiglaf

uncertainly. He had never gone into the heart of the Dark Forest. Everyone knew it was full of strange creatures, fierce trolls, and crazy hermits.

"I'm for taking the shortcut," said Janice. "It'll be a fun adventure!"

"Et's-lay o-gay!" said Daisy.

Wiglaf could not believe his pig had just said, "Let's go!" He was scared to take the shortcut. But if his pig was not afraid, how could he admit that he was?

"Are you sure, Daisy?" Wiglaf asked.

Daisy nodded. *"Y-may egs-lay are-yay oo-tay ort-shay or-fay ong-lay alks-way."*

"What did she say?" asked Janice. "I don't understand Pig Latin."

"She said, 'My legs are too short for long walks,'" Wiglaf told Janice.

"Forget it!" said Angus. "I shall not set foot in the creepy Dark Forest. We might run into the headless executioner. Or a gang of nasty elves. Or a monster!"

"Yet, if we take the shortcut," Erica said, "we shall reach the palace by suppertime... cherry pie with whipping cream!"

"What are we waiting for?" cried Angus. He ran up the path, across the Stone Bridge, and into the forest.

The moment Wiglaf stepped into the Dark Forest, his heart began to beat faster. The light was dim, for the sun could not shine through the tangled branches overhead. Trees and bushes took on eerie shapes.

"Ughhh," Erica grunted. "All these roots in the path make pulling my trunk very hard."

"Let me have a turn," said Janice. She took the trunk handle from Erica.

Just then Wiglaf spied a cave.

"Look, Erica!" he exclaimed. "Was that not Gorzil's cave?"

"'Twas!" exclaimed Erica. "That is where Wiggie and I slew a vicious dragon!" she told

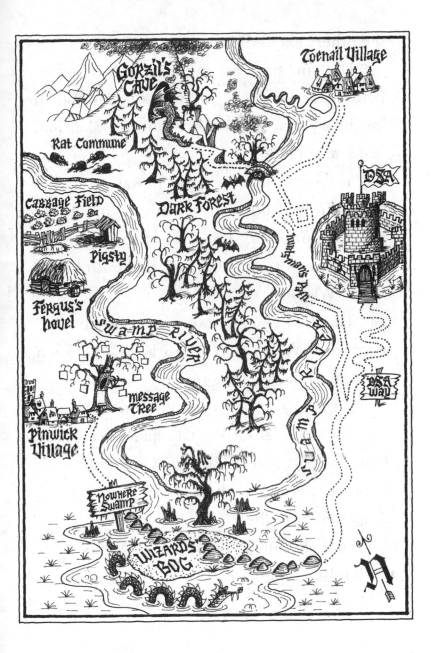

the others excitedly.

"Did you slash him and bash him?" asked Janice eagerly. She began whacking away at an imaginary dragon with her lance. "Take that, you scaly fiend!"

"Yes!" exclaimed Erica. "It was a terrible battle. Gorzil shot flames from his snout. He belched up red-hot lava. But at last I stabbed him in the gut, and that was the end of him. Right, Wiggie?"

"That is not *exactly* the way I remember it," muttered Wiglaf. For in truth, he had been the one to slay the dragon.

Every dragon has a secret fatal weakness, and by accident, Wiglaf had discovered Gorzil's—bad jokes. He told Gorzil some of Fergus's awful knock-knock jokes, and the dragon had laughed himself to death.

"Enough dillydallying," said Angus. "Or we'll miss supper."

Erica took her trunk back from Janice.

Then on they went, over rocks and roots, deeper and deeper into the Dark Forest.

"*O-say ired-tay,*" Daisy murmured.

"What did she say?" asked Janice.

" 'So tired,' " said Wiglaf.

"I wish I could understand you, Daisy," Janice said. "Can you teach me Pig Latin?"

"*All-yay ight-ray,*" said Daisy happily.

"She's saying 'all right.'" said Wiglaf.

They all sat down on a log.

"*Art-stay ith-way ames-nay,*" said Daisy.

"Huh?" said Janice.

"She said, 'Start with names,'" Wiglaf explained.

Daisy pointed a hoof and said, "*Anice-jay.*"

"That's me?" said Janice.

Wiglaf nodded. "Here is the trick. Say your name without the *J* at the beginning."

"Anice," said Janice.

"Now take the *J* and add it to '-ay.' It becomes 'jay.' Then put them together."

"Anice...jay?" said Janice. *"Anice-jay!"*

"Ight-ray!" said Wiglaf. "Now try Wiglaf."

"Iglaf," said Janice. *"Iglaf-way."* Her face lit up. "I'm speaking Pig Latin!" She turned to Daisy and said, "Daisy—*Aisy-day!*"

"My name is different," said Angus.

"For words that start with *A, E, I, O,* or *U,*" said Wiglaf, "you simply say the word and add '-yay' at the end."

"Angus-yay?" said Janice. She turned to Erica. *"Erica-yay?"*

"Ou-yay ot-gay it-yay," said Daisy.

"You...got...it," said Janice. "Hey, I do!"

"Say 'troll' in Pig Latin," said Wiglaf.

Janice frowned. *"Oll-tray?"*

"Erfect-pay," said Daisy.

"Et's-lay et-gay oing-gay," said Angus.

"Tell us about the palace," said Wiglaf as they trooped on.

"It has many white marble towers and sits high on a hill overlooking a large park," said Erica.

Wiglaf tried to imagine such a splendid sight. It sounded like a palace in a fairy tale.

"My mother's herd of wild black unicorns lives in the park," Erica went on. "They have red horns and can run like the wind."

Erica suddenly stopped short. "Oh, I just remembered!" she cried. "Tomorrow marks twenty-five years that my father has been king! Popsy gives a speech every year on the anniversary of his crowning. After that, there's always a feast."

"A feast!" cried Angus. "Zounds!"

Then he did something most unusual for Angus—he started running. He had not gone far when the toe of his boot caught on a tree root, and he pitched forward. "Oof!" he cried as he hit the forest floor with a great thud.

Chapter 3

veryone rushed to Angus.

"Are you hurt?" Wiglaf cried.

"Yeeeees!" wailed Angus. He sat up, holding his knee. His leggings were ripped, and his knee was bleeding badly. Tears ran down his dirt-streaked cheeks.

Wiglaf turned his face away—the sight of blood made him sick.

"Fie!" exclaimed Erica. "My Sir Lancelot first-aid kit is back at DSA."

"Oor-pay Angus-yay," said Daisy.

"'Poor Angus' is right," Angus whimpered. He got up and tried to walk but limped badly. "Now we shall never make it to the palace in time for supper!" He began to weep harder.

"There are always lots of leftovers," said Erica. "Now, the important thing is to clean your wound."

"Noooo!" wailed Angus, covering his knee with his hand. "It will hurt!"

"But less than if your wound festers and your leg must be cut off," Janice pointed out.

Blech! Wiglaf felt dizzy and held on to a tree trunk.

Angus looked horrified. But he uncovered his knee.

Wiglaf was the only one with water left in his flask. He tried not to gag as he helped rinse off Angus's bloody knee. Afterward, he gave his share of Brother Dave's peanut brittle to Angus to comfort him.

"You are a true friend," said Angus. He popped the whole piece into his mouth.

Daisy peered at his wound. "*Ungo-jay eaves-lay,*" she muttered. Then she trotted off into the forest.

"I didn't catch that," said Janice.

"'Jungo leaves,'" said Wiglaf. "I know not what it means. Yet Daisy knows a great deal about almost everything. Brother Dave is always bringing her library books."

Erica added, "Daisy is very wise. She was our coach when DSA entered the All-School Brain-Power Tournament."

"Forget the tournament!" cried Angus. "What about my knee?" He pulled himself to his feet. Once again, he tried to take a few steps, but it hurt too much. "Ow! Ow!" he cried, and sat back down.

"Daisy is getting something to help," said Wiglaf. "Listen—I hear footsteps. She must be coming back already."

Everyone listened. They heard the sound of feet on the path. Heavy feet.

"Those are not Daisy's footsteps," Wiglaf whispered. Someone—or something—much bigger than his pig was coming toward them through the forest.

Erica leaped up. She drew her sword. "Who goes there?" she cried.

No one answered.

The footsteps grew louder.

Janice jumped up and grabbed her lance. "This is so exciting!" she whispered.

Wiglaf stood, too. He took Surekill from his pack. He would never harm any living creature. Still, he hoped he might scare whatever it was away.

"Make yourself known!" yelled Erica. "Or we dragon slayers shall run you through!"

"No, please!" came a quavery voice. "I come in peace."

A plump, white-haired woman stepped into the clearing. She wore a long gray dress and carried a bulging bag.

"Albon is my name," said the old one. "Alchemy is my game."

"Alchemy?" said Wiglaf. "You mean you

can make gold?"

"Correct!" said Albon. "Tin, brass, iron, you name it. I can take any ordinary metal and turn it into gold. And I'm not talking gold plate, either. I'm talking pure, twenty-four-karat gold." Her blue eyes sparkled. "I am on my way to an alchemists' convention. But sadly, I have lost my way." She reached into her bag and pulled out a piece of parchment. "Can one of you, perchance, help me out?"

Erica took the parchment just as Daisy came trotting back. Everybody looked at it together.

"I cannot believe this!" exclaimed Wiglaf.

"Let me see it!" cried Angus.

Janice handed him the flyer.

Now it was Angus's turn to read:

COME YE, COME YE
TO THE ALCHEMY CONVENTION
Friday, Saturday, and Sunday
AT DRAGON SLAYERS' RESORT HOTEL

(on DSA Way, just off Huntsman's Path)
**SEE AMAZING GOLD-MAKING DEMONSTRATIONS!
**LEARN ANCIENT GOLD-MAKING SECRETS!
**SHARE GOLD-MAKING TRICKS WITH FELLOW ALCHEMISTS!
Luxurious Accommodations
at bargain rates if you pay up front in
GOLD!
RSVP to Mordred de Marvelous
or just show up.
But don't forget to bring your GOLD.

"Madam," said Erica. "Dragon Slayers' is no resort hotel. It is a school."

"*Our* school," said Janice.

"Ha!" cried Angus. "I knew there was something fishy about Uncle Mordred giving us a holiday. He just wanted to get rid of us so he could rent out our cots!"

Chapter 4

s soon as Albon was on her way, Daisy showed Wiglaf the herbs she'd found.

"Ake-tay is-thay, Iglaf-way," she said. In the cleft of her right front hoof she carried a leafy bouquet.

Wiglaf took the leaves. Daisy told him to rub them together to warm them, then press them onto Angus's knee.

Wiglaf did so quickly.

"Ow!" said Angus. "Get those weeds off my wound!"

"Ealing-hay erbs-hay," said Daisy.

"Healing herbs, poppycock!" cried Angus. "I don't see how a bunch of—" He paused. A look of surprise crossed his face. "Hey, wait a minute. My knee doesn't hurt anymore!"

Daisy nodded knowingly. Wiglaf felt so proud of his pig.

Minutes later, Daisy told Angus to peel off the leaves. His wound had stopped bleeding. Now it was hardly more than a scratch.

Angus stood up. He bent his knee, then straightened it. "Daisy, you are a genius. An *enius-gay!*" he cried. "I'm ready to go!"

The little band started off again.

"How did you know about jungo leaves, Daisy?" Angus asked as they walked.

"I-yay ave-hay ead-ray any-may ooks-bay on-yay ealing-hay erbs-hay," Daisy said.

"Did you say, 'I have read many books on healing herbs'?" Janice asked.

Daisy nodded.

"Whoopie! I got it!" cried Janice. "I know a foreign language!"

As they trekked on, the path grew steeper. It became littered with big chunks of stone.

"Fie! These broken rocks!" cried Erica. "They are murder on my trunk's wheels."

The jagged rocks also made it harder for Daisy to walk. So Angus, feeling grateful for her doctoring, picked her up and carried her.

Wiglaf saw a small troll peek out from between two pine trees. A bird screamed above him. Or was it a bat? He heard hermits shouting, "Leave me alone!" Then he heard a new noise: singing.

"Do you hear that?" he whispered.

The others nodded.

The singing grew louder. Soon Wiglaf could make out the words of the song:

> *Gorzil was a dragon, a greedy one was he,*
> *From his jaws of terror, villagers did flee.*

"Gorzil?" said Janice. She turned to Erica. "Is that not the dragon you and Wiglaf slew?"

Erica nodded.

"I—I once knew a minstrel who sang such a song," said Wiglaf.

Just then a man in a feathered cap stepped onto the path before them, strumming a lute and singing to himself. He looked up.

"Can it be?" he exclaimed. "Wiglaf of Pinwick?"

Wiglaf gasped. "Minstrel! How glad I am to see you!"

Wiglaf introduced the minstrel to his friends. He told them how the minstrel had come to Pinwick during a winter snowstorm. He needed a place to stay and, for a while, lived in their pigsty.

"Hello, Daisy!" said the minstrel, looking down at the pig. "Still the finest, pinkest pig in all the land."

Daisy blushed, turning even pinker.

"The minstrel taught me how to read and write," Wiglaf said. "And how to wiggle my ears." He gave a little demonstration.

"News of your deeds has reached me, Wiglaf," said the minstrel. "You slew Gorzil and Seetha!"

"Both by accident," Wiglaf confessed.

"Be not so modest." The minstrel smiled. "I said you were born to be a mighty hero."

Wiglaf felt his face grow warm.

"I have just put you into one of my songs," said the minstrel. He strummed and sang:

> *Gorzil was a dragon, a greedy one was he,*
> *From his jaws of terror, villagers did flee.*
> *Gorzil burped up clouds of smoke,*
> *Shot lightning from his snout,*
> *Then one day came a hero,*
> *Who found his secret out.*
> *The hero's name is Wiglaf.*
> *He's small yet he is bold.*
> *He slew the dragon Gorzil,*
> *With knock-knocks knocked him cold!*

Everyone clapped.

Erica muttered, "That's not exactly the way I remember it." But she clapped, too.

The minstrel swept off his feathered cap and bowed.

"Thank you, Minstrel," Wiglaf said. "'Tis a fine honor to be in your song."

"Do you really tell fortunes?" asked Janice.

"That I do," said the minstrel. "Hold out your palm, lass." He traced its lines with his finger. "Let me see now...this crease crosses that line. Hmmm. Oh, wait. I see it clearly now. Very soon you shall meet a wizard."

"Oh, boy!" Janice turned to Erica. "Why did you not tell us there is a wizard at the palace?"

"Because there isn't one." Erica shrugged. "My fairy godmother used to keep a small apartment in the palace, but she left for good when I turned five."

"If I am wrong," said the minstrel, "it will be the first time."

"My turn." Angus held out his hand.

"What a nice plump palm!" exclaimed the wizard. He studied it for a while and said, "You shall say nay to fresh-baked pie."

"Never!" cried Angus. "Pie is my favorite dessert—especially cherry pie."

"I read what I see," the minstrel said. "In truth, I do not always understand it myself."

Erica held out her palm.

The minstrel hardly seemed to glance at it. "Clear as a bell," he said. "You shall see spots before your eyes."

"Spots?" Erica looked annoyed. "That, Minstrel, is not much of a fortune."

Wiglaf knew that Erica had hoped to hear the minstrel say she would become a great hero like Sir Lancelot. But seeing spots? He agreed with Erica. It was not much of a fortune.

Now Daisy stepped up to the minstrel and

held up her right front hoof.

"Daisy, dear pig," the minstrel said. "I am a palm reader. But if you wish me to read your hoof, well, why not?" He held her hoof in his hand. He bent close to examine it. His eyes grew suddenly wide. He took a step back, dropping Daisy's hoof.

"Egad-yay!" cried Daisy. *"Is-yay it-yay ad-bay?"*

The minstrel looked worried.

"What did you see, Minstrel?" cried Wiglaf.

"I saw..." the minstrel began. But he stopped and smiled a shaky smile. "Prithee, a hoof is not a palm. I saw nothing." He picked up his lute. "I must go," he said. "And quickly. Or I shall be late for the Toenail Fair."

He bent toward Wiglaf. "Keep a close eye on your pig," he whispered. Then he turned and called, "Farewell! Farewell!" and headed east on the rocky path.

"Farewell, Minstrel!" Wiglaf called back.

He knelt down and put his arms around his pig. What fortune had the minstrel seen in Daisy's hoof? He shivered. He could not stand it if anything should happen to his dear Daisy.

Chapter 5

Wiglaf's spirits were low as he and the others trooped on through the Dark Forest. *Was this a shortcut?* he wondered. It seemed more like a longcut.

Then, without warning, a raspy voice spoke from behind a clump of bushes: "Sssssssssssssstop!"

Wiglaf's heart began to pound. He clutched Daisy to him.

"Who—who said that?" called Erica.

"The name issss Basssil," said the voice. "I need assssisssstancccce."

"Show yourself!" said Janicc. "Then we shall decide if we will help you."

"Ah, that issss a problem," said Basil. "For

if you sssssee me, you shall perish."

"Perish?" squeaked Wiglaf. "As in *die?*"

"Yessss," said Basil. "That issss correct. You will die. For I am a bassssilissssk. Perhapssssss you have heard of my kind?"

"I have," said Wiglaf. He had checked out every book on monsters in the DSA library. "You have a scaly body, short legs, clawed feet, wings too small for flying, a long tail, and the head of a chicken."

"I prefer 'head of a roossssster,' " said Basil. "But you got the resssst right. And what issss your name?"

"Wiglaf," said Wiglaf. "If a basilisk steps on a stone," he went on, "the stone splits in two."

"Insssstantly," said Basil.

"So that explains all the broken rocks we saw," said Erica.

"Basilisks have a great treasure, known as Basilisk Gold," Wiglaf continued.

"Yesssss," said Basil proudly. "We bassssilissssks are very rich."

The basilisk also had really bad breath, but Wiglaf felt it would be rude to mention it.

"Let me get this straight," said Angus. "If we look at you, we die?"

"Ssssadly sssso," said Basil. "And the sssssame ssssad fate awaitssss any creature I look upon—except for another bassssilissssk."

"Egad!" cried Wiglaf.

"Don't be sssscared," said Basil. "I wear dark glassssessss sssso my sssstare won't hurt you."

"Oh, good," Angus said in a shaky voice. "Keep those glasses on, Basil."

"I wandered into the Dark Foresssst by missssstake," Basil went on. "With thessssse glasssssessssss on, I cannot sssssee a thing, sssso I am losssst. If you will kindly lead me out of the foressst, I shall be able to find my dear Sssssophie."

"Who is Sophie?" asked Wiglaf.

"Ssssophie isssss a beautiful bassssilissssk," said Basil. "Too bad it would kill you to sssee her. The feathered cressst on her head issss ssssssspectacular."

"I have a rope with me," said Wiglaf. "If you hold one end while we walk ahead, I can lead you out of the forest."

"You are a geniussss, Wiglaf!" cried Basil.

Wiglaf held one end of the rope and walked ahead with the others. He felt a tug.

"Got it!" called Basil from behind. "Promisssse to sssstay with me until we get out of the Dark Foresssst?"

"I promise," said Wiglaf.

Wiglaf led the basilisk through the murky Dark Forest. At last they came to a bridge. Far below roared the Swamp River.

"Here we are at the Swinging Bridge!" said Erica. "Once we cross it, we shall be out of the Dark Forest. And very near the palace."

"Yay!" cried Angus. "Supper time!"

Wiglaf squinted at the bridge through the dim light. Why, it was no more than wooden planks set across ropes. He took a few steps closer. He saw that the wooden planks looked rotten, and the ropes were frayed.

"Here I go!" said Erica. The bridge swung wildly as she went across, her heavy trunk bumping along behind her.

Wiglaf shut his eyes. He could hear planks cracking and breaking. "Be careful," he told Janice, who went next.

"I can use my lance for balance," she said. But as she teetered across—*Crrrrack*! More of the planks split in two and plummeted into the racing river below.

Angus stepped up to the bridge. He gulped, then drew a deep breath. "Cherry pie and whipping cream...cherry pie and whipping cream," he chanted as he made his way across.

Daisy trotted over the bridge behind him.

Now it was Wiglaf's turn. Half of the bridge was gone. He took a deep breath. "Ready, Basil?" he said.

"I'm sssscared," Basil said from behind. "The bridge will sssnap under ussss. And my wingssss are usssselessss, sssso I cannot fly. We will have to crosssssss thissssss river ssssome other way."

"But the only other way is to...swim," said Wiglaf.

"Very well," said Basil. "We shall sssswim. But I cannot ssssee, remember? You will have to ride on my back and be my eyessss."

"Ride...on your back?" cried Wiglaf.

"No, Wiggie!" Erica cried out to him from the far side of the river. "Don't do it! It is too dangerous!"

How Wiglaf wanted to dash across the bridge to his friends! Yet he had promised the basilisk. He could not leave him stranded in the Dark Forest. In a shaky voice he said, "Let us swim, Basil."

"We'll be on the riverbank!" called Erica.

Wiglaf's friends ran down to the river.

"Closssse your eyessss, Wiglaf," Basil said.

Wiglaf closed his eyes. His heart was racing. He felt the cold scaly monster come up beside him. He managed to throw a leg over the basilisk's back.

"Hold on to my neck," said Basil.

Wiglaf put his arms around the basilisk's neck. It felt dry and scaly, like Worm's neck. Thinking of the young dragon calmed him. He held on tight.

Basil lumbered down to the river's edge.

"Brrrr!" he said. "It'ssss freezzzing! Only a lovesssick fool would do thissss! Ssssophie, sssssweetheart, here I come!"

SPLASH! Basil plunged into the dark waters

of the Swamp River. Wiglaf felt the basilisk paddling like a dog in the swift current. His eyes popped open. At first all he could see was splashing water. Then he sat up straighter, peering ahead, and saw the shore.

"Yikes!" cried Wiglaf. "We're drifting downstream. Swim to the right, Basil. Swim!"

Basil paddled madly to the right.

"Hold steady now!" Wiglaf shouted.

Basil basilisk-paddled on. At last they reached the far shore.

"Ssssafe at lasssst!" cried Basil as he lumbered out of the water and onto dry land.

Wiglaf closed his eyes and slid off the basilisk's back.

"Thank you, Wiglaf," said Basil. "Now I shall go find Sssophie."

"Farewell, Basil," said Wiglaf, keeping his back to the basilisk. "I wish I could see you."

"Me too," said Basil. "I am a very

handsssssome bassssilisssk. At leassst that issss what Ssssophie ssssays. If we have a brood of bassssilisssk chickssss, I shall sssuggesssst that we name one after you."

Wiglaf smiled. A little monster named Wiglaf!

He kept his eyes closed, listening as Basil scuttled away. Then all was quiet.

"Basil?" he called. "Are you here?"

No answer came.

Wiglaf opened his eyes. The basilisk was gone. His own rope lay coiled at his feet. And inside the coil lay a six-sided golden coin. A piece of Basilisk Gold!

Chapter 6

"Is the coast clear?" asked Erica, popping up from behind a bush.

"Yes," said Wiglaf. "Basil has gone. And look what he left behind."

Erica and the others turned around. They stared at the gold coin.

Angus gasped. "It must be worth a fortune!"

"There is something special about Basilisk Gold," Wiglaf said. *It had to do with "twenty-four,"* he thought as he picked up the coin. *Did only twenty-four basilisks know where the Basilisk Gold was hidden? Or maybe the coins were pure, 24-karat gold, like the gold that Albon the Alchemist made.* Wiglaf could not quite remember.

One side of the coin showed a roosterlike head. The other, a clawed foot standing atop a cracking rock. Wiglaf slipped the coin into his pocket. Just as Brother Dave had predicted, this was turning out to be a wondrous journey indeed.

"*Iglaf-way,*" said Daisy as they scrambled back up the hill. "*Ou-yay ere-way ery-vay ave-bray.*"

"Thank you, Daisy," said Wiglaf, happy to have his wise pig think him brave.

"Look!" said Erica as they reached the top of the hill. "There's the palace!"

Wiglaf shaded his eyes from the afternoon sun. In the distance, he saw sparkling white towers rising up to meet the sky.

"This trunk is going downhill on its own," said Erica. She set it down and gave it a shove. The trunk bumped down the hillside, picking up speed as it rolled.

"Let's roll too!" said Janice.

Four future dragon slayers and one pig flung themselves onto the grass and rolled down the hill. At the bottom, they brushed the grass off, found Erica's trunk, and started off on the road to the palace.

Along the way, they passed peasants going about their business. Wiglaf overheard some of them talking.

"King Ken is turning into a bloody fool, if you ask me," said a woman in a white wimple.

"Always has been thick as a plank," said a man in a leather jerkin. "I want a king I can be proud of—not one who's famous for setting fire to his breeches."

Wiglaf glanced at Erica to see if she had heard these comments. It was her father they were talking about!

But Erica only rolled her eyes. "Peasants always complain about royals," she said. "That's just the way it is."

Wiglaf wondered—had Erica forgotten that he was a peasant?

A peasant woman in blue spoke up. "I hear King Ken's come down with a mysterious illness."

"King Bob of Bobbinshire is a proper monarch," said a red-nosed man in grimy leggings. "If anything happens to King Ken, maybe he could be our king."

Erica frowned. "Peasants love nothing better than spreading ridiculous rumors about the royal family," she said. Yet she picked up the pace. Soon they came to an iron gate in the high stone wall surrounding the palace.

"Guards!" Erica called through the iron bars. "It is I—Princess Erica Wilamina Bernadette Paula Frieda Marie von Royale!"

Wiglaf had no idea that Erica had so many middle names!

A guard in a bright red uniform ran over to the gate. He peered at Erica. Then he turned

and disappeared into the guardhouse.

"He must be new," Erica said. "Anyway, I have been breaking in since I was three." With that, she boosted herself onto the iron gate, reached through the bars, and fiddled with the lock. *Boing!* The gates sprang open.

A minute later, Wiglaf of Pinwick was walking around the palace grounds. He could hardly believe it! Ahead he saw hedges trimmed to look like dragons.

"The dragons were my idea," said Erica. "They look very scary in the moonlight."

"Zounds, Erica!" exclaimed Wiglaf. "How could you ever leave this palace?"

"It is a fine place for a princess," she said. "But not for a dragon-slayer-in-training."

Wiglaf caught sight of a fountain. Gold-tinted water spurted high into the air. Goldfish the size of rabbits swam around in the fountain's pool.

"The Royal Goldfish Pond," Erica said.

"Hello, Lancelot!" She dabbled her fingers in the water in front of a large goldfish. "Those two are Arthur and Guinevere."

"Princess Erica!" someone called.

Wiglaf looked up. A blue-uniformed servant was barreling down the palace steps, bowing as he ran.

"Hello, Fawnsley," said Erica as the servant reached her.

"I *am* sorry to be the bearer of bad news, Princess Erica." Fawnsley bowed again. "But there is trouble in the palace. Trouble, I tell you. Oh, woe is us!"

Erica frowned. "What do you mean, Fawnsley? Stop bowing and spit it out!"

"Your father the king—ouch!" Fawnsley had bowed too low and banged his nose on the ground. "Has come down with the pox!"

"So it was not a rumor after all!" cried Erica. "I must go to my father at once!"

"Oh, no, Princess!" Fawnsley bowed. "He

will see no one. He is fevered and his royal face is covered with liver-colored spots. His royal hands and his royal arms, too. The royal whole of him, really."

Wiglaf glanced at Daisy. "Are there any herbs that will get rid of pox?" he asked her.

"*Ertainly-cay,*" said Daisy.

"Sixteen doctors have come to cure the king," Fawnsley said, bowing. "And sixteen have failed. Number seventeen is on his way."

"Where is my mother, Fawnsley?" said Erica. "I must speak to her now!"

"The queen—" Fawnsley bowed, "—has gone to fetch a wizard. She has heard that wizards work wonders with the pox."

Now Daisy stepped up to Fawnsley. "*Ake-tay e-may o-tay e-thay ing-kay,*" she said. "*I-yay an-cay elp-hay im-hay.*"

"Egad!" cried Fawnsley. "Did the swine speak? Or am I losing my marbles?"

"'Twas the pig," said Erica.

"She asks you to take her to the king," added Wiglaf. "She says she can help him."

Fawnsley's mouth dropped open in surprise. "A p-p-pig?" he sputtered. "Help the k-k-king?" This thought was too much for Fawnsley. His eyes rolled back, and he fainted dead away.

Chapter 7

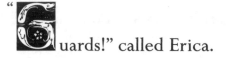uards!" called Erica.

Two red-coated guards trotted over to her and saluted.

"See to Fawnsley!" she commanded.

No wonder Erica was so bossy, Wiglaf thought. *She was used to giving orders. And used to being obeyed.* The guards picked Fawnsley up under his arms and dragged him away.

Erica beckoned her friends. "Come! Let us go to my father," she said.

The group hurried after her up the steps and into the palace. They rushed through room after room, passing red-coated guards, blue-uniformed servants, and lovely young maidens in lacy silken dresses. Wiglaf stared at them in wonder.

"Are they princesses, too?" he asked.

"They are ladies-in-waiting," said Erica. "*I am the only princess around here.*"

Erica led them up a wide staircase and down a hallway. At the end of it, Wiglaf heard someone groaning.

Erica pushed open a golden door and ran into the chamber, calling, "Popsy!"

The others stepped into the room. It was vast—ten times the size of Wiglaf's whole hovel in Pinwick. The king lay in a great canopy bed at the far end of the chamber.

"Woe!" he cried, staring into a looking glass. "Woe is I!"

Even from a distance, Wiglaf could see that the king was covered with pox.

"Can you help him, Daisy?" Wiglaf asked.

"*Erhaps-pay,*" she whispered.

The king lowered his looking glass. "I say!" he cried. "Is that you, Poppet?"

Erica hugged him. "Yes, Popsy!" she said.

"I am be-poxed!" wailed the king. He held up the looking glass again. "Oh, fie! A new pox is popping up on my nose!"

Daisy trotted up to the king's bed.

"Ood-gay ay-day, Our-yay Oyal-ray Ighness-hay," she said.

"Gadzooks!" cried the king again. "I thought I heard the pig speak!"

Wiglaf stepped forward. "You did, sire," he said. "Her name is Daisy and she said, 'Good day, Your Royal Highness.' "

"Good day?" The king glanced again into the looking glass. "Not for me, it isn't."

"Daisy may be of help to you, sire," said Wiglaf. "She knows how to get rid of pox."

"She knows all about healing herbs, Popsy," added Erica.

"Isterwort-blay is-yay est-bay," Daisy said.

"Blisterwort is best," Wiglaf translated.

"I say!" said King Ken. "Has Fawnsley sent

me a pig doctor?"

Suddenly the door opened again.

"Never fear!" cried a man in a black cloak and wide-brimmed black hat. He carried a black box. "Dr. Leechworth is here!" He rushed over to the king. "Everybody out!" he shouted. "And take that filthy swine with you."

"Not so fast," said Erica. "How do we know you are a good doctor?"

"I cured the Prince of Sneezblastia's hay fever," said Dr. Leechworth. "I removed warts from the Queen of Toadsgrabia. I took out the Duchess of Strepthroatsia's tonsils! And now I will cure King Ken's pox!"

"How?" asked Erica.

Dr. Leechworth smiled and held up his black box. "I have here the world's most advanced medicine," he said, setting the box on the king's bedside table. He opened it. Dozens of little snakelike heads popped up.

"Down, boys," said the doctor. "Patience! You shall all get a taste of the king."

"What *are* those things?" cried Angus.

"Leeches," said the doctor. "They will draw out the king's bad blood. Then his pox will disappear. He will be cured!"

Leeches? Wiglaf's stomach lurched, and his head swam as he looked at the slimy, black bloodsuckers. The thought of one of them touching his skin made him go weak in the knees.

The doctor lifted a thin leech from the box. "You may feel a tiny sting," he told the king as he put the leech on his cheek.

"Yowie!" cried the king. "It bit me!"

Wiglaf closed his eyes. He felt very sick and very, very sorry for the king!

"Are—are you sure leeches will help, doctor?" cried Erica.

"Yes," said Dr. Leechworth.

"O-nay," said Daisy.

But no one was playing attention to her.

Every eye but Wiglaf's was fastened on the doctor as the man quickly dealt out more leeches. He put a dozen on the king's chest. Several more on each shoulder. One on his forehead. Another on his big toe.

"Look," said Janice. "The leeches are turning blue."

Wiglaf opened one eye and was instantly sorry. Gaaach! The leeches had bloated up and turned the color of a bad bruise.

"Shouldn't they be turning red from sucking blood?" asked Angus.

"Ignorant peasant!" muttered the doctor. "Royals have blue blood."

"And I want to keep some of mine!" cried the king, who was covered in fat, blue leeches.

"Almost finished," said the doctor.

"Yoo-hoo, Kenny!" cried a voice from the

doorway. "I'm home!"

"Mumsy!" cried Erica, running to her.

"Darling!" cried Queen Barb, giving her a hug. "What a nice surprise! And you've brought your friends. And, oh!" The queen's eyebrows shot up. "A piggy! I am having a day of surprises. Chef Pierre just told me that he can't find a single pheasant for tomorrow's feast. So! You've seen your poor Popsy, darling. Awful, isn't it?"

Erica nodded. "Terrible!"

The queen lowered her voice. "I'm letting only a few trusted guards and servants see him," she said. "I hope they won't talk. And I trust your friends shan't either."

"Never!" said Erica.

The queen sighed. "Your father has been king for twenty-five years," she said. "Our subjects are coming to the palace tomorrow night to hear his Silver Anniversary speech. I've been working with him on it night and day. I want everyone to see what a good, kind king he is—that he's not just some fool who set fire to his pants." She pulled out a lace hankie and sniffed into it. "If our subjects see Kenny covered with a strange pox, why, they might banish us from the kingdom."

Wiglaf remembered the peasants he had overheard on the way to the palace. The queen was right to worry.

"Your father must be poxfree by tomorrow so he can make his speech," the queen went on. "That's why I went to fetch a world-famous wizard."

Probably Zizmor, the head wizard, Wiglaf thought to himself.

"Hallo, Babsie," the king called weakly.

The queen rushed over to the king's bedside. "What are those disgusting *things* all over you?" she cried.

"Leeches, Your Highness," said Dr. Leechworth. "Allow me to introduce myself—"

"I don't care who you are," said the queen. "Get those big fat suckers off the king, or I'm calling the royal executioner."

Dr. Leechworth worked fast. He grabbed a swollen blue leech and yanked. *POP!* Off it came, spewing blue blood in all directions.

Wiglaf gagged. Blue blood made him even sicker than common red blood! He clapped a hand over his mouth and tried to think of something—anything!—besides the bloody scene before him.

POP! POP! POP! POP! POP!

The doctor tried stuffing his leeches back into his black box, but now they were too full and fat to fit. He took off his wide-brimmed hat and dumped leeches into it.

"Oh, my poor Kenny!" wailed Queen Barb. She whirled around and glared at Dr. Leechworth. "Be gone, varlet!"

The doctor quickly picked up his box and, forgetting about the leeches, put on his hat.

The slimy creatures oozed out, slid down his face, and attached themselves to his neck.

"Owwww," squealed the doctor as he ran from the room. "That hurts!"

Queen Barb turned to her pale, spotty husband. She stroked his forehead. "Hold on, Kenny," she said. "The wizard is freshening up. He'll be here any minute. And he shall cure you of these horrid pox."

"I say," murmured the king.

The queen beckoned Erica and her friends to come closer to the king's bed.

"Kenny, darling," she said, plumping his pillow. "Why don't you practice your speech for Poppet and her friends?"

King Ken sat up in bed. "Ladies and laddies!" he said.

"Ladies and gentlemen," corrected the queen.

"Ah," said the king. "Ladies and gentlemen! Villagers and pheasants!"

"That's 'peasants,' dear," said the queen.

The king nodded and went on. "In honor of the twenty-fifth anniversary of my carnation—"

"It's 'coronation,'" said the queen. "A 'carnation' is a flower."

"Ah, so it is," said the king. He began again. "I, Your Royal Highness have ordered up," the king went on, "a walloping big feast."

Just then a tall wizard with wild white hair raced into the king's chamber. "Here I come to save the king!" he sang. He wore a blue robe dotted with stars. "Show me a pox-covered king, Your Queenly Highniness. And I'll show you what wizardry is all about!"

"Egad!" cried Wiglaf when he saw who the wizard was.

The queen had brought home Zelnoc!

Chapter 8

"Oh, jester's bells!" exclaimed Zelnoc as he looked around the chamber. "The whole gang's here. Even the porker."

"Orker-pay?" Daisy glared at the wizard.

"Where's Zizmor?" asked Erica. "Why are *you* here?"

"Darling, do you know this wizard?" the queen asked Erica.

But before Erica could answer, Zelnoc rushed over to the king. "Hmm. This looks very bad. I'll chant the spell right now." He cleared his throat. "Oh, bats and belfries! My voice is hoarse."

"Don't worry, wizard," said the queen. "I shall fetch you a glass of water myself." She hurried from the chamber.

As soon as her mother was gone, Erica said, "Have a snooze, Popsy. We'll be right back." She herded her friends and the wizard into her father's dressing room and shut the door behind them.

"Zelnoc!" she whispered. "What are you up to?"

"Zizmor was busy," said Zelnoc. "So I'm here to heal the king."

"Will someone please tell me what's going on?" cried Janice.

"This is Zelnoc," Wiglaf told her. "His spells, well, um—they do not always turn out right."

"At's-thay y-whay I-yay alk-tay ike-lay is-thay!" added Daisy.

"Be gone, wizard!" said Erica. "My father has enough troubles without you messing up a spell and changing him into a dragon."

"Are you referring to that time I turned

you three into dragons?" Zelnoc asked. He shrugged. "Big deal. So I made one mistake. Besides, I'll bet you had loads of fun flying around."

"How about your Ghost-Be-Gone Spell?" said Angus. "That was supposed to get rid of a ghost. Instead, it summoned one."

"So I brought one measly ghost to DSA," said Zelnoc. "Okay. Two mistakes. Everyone has a bad day now and then—even a wizard. But hey! Third time's a charm. I *can* cure the king."

Erica shook her head. "Do not even *think* about putting a spell on my father."

"Oh, please, Princess!" wailed the wizard. He fell to his knobby knees. "Have pity on a poor spell-caster who's down on his luck. My Get-Well Spell is foolproof. The king will be poxfree in minutes if you'll only give me one little chance."

"Really and truly?" said Erica.

"Do bats have wings?" cried Zelnoc, popping up again. "I guarantee it 150 percent. Oh, it would be such a feather in my cap if I could tell Zizmor that I was a King Healer. Why, Ziz might even put me on the Decorations Committee for the big Wizards' Weekend. I've been doing cleanup for the last 472 years!"

Wiglaf knew how Zelnoc felt. He'd been doing kitchen cleanup since he arrived at DSA. But could they trust this crazy wizard?

"I say!" King Ken called from his bed. "My pox are itching! Come out of there and let the wizard have a go."

Erica stepped up close to the wizard. "All right. Try it," she said. "But we shall be watching you—just in case."

They came out of the dressing room.

Zelnoc stood beside the king's bed. He drew his wand out of his left sleeve. "Everyone keep quiet," he said. "I must not be disturbed while I cast this spell." He raised his wand and began to chant:

> Oh spotted king, you bet your socks,
> That I can disappear your pox,
> For when I count from one to three,
> Of socks and pox you shall be free!

Zelnoc waved his wand over King Ken and shouted, *"One!"*

Next, Zelnoc touched the wand to his own forehead and shouted, *"Two!"*

Zelnoc had just touched his wand to the king's forehead when the door flew open.

"Here's your water, Wizard!" called the queen.

The startled wizard whirled around. His wand flew out of his hand, hitting Daisy on the head, as he shouted out, *"Three!"*

King Ken's socks shot across the room.

"Good heavens!" cried Queen Barb.

"Daisy!" Wiglaf cried. "Are you hurt?"

Daisy rubbed her head and looked up at Wiglaf. She shook her head. But Wiglaf thought she looked quite pale.

"Popsy!" cried Erica. "Your pox are gone!"

"They are, Kenny!" cried Queen Barb. "All gone! You're cured!"

Wiglaf glanced at the king. Sure enough, he was poxfree.

"What did I tell you?" cried Zelnoc.

"Here's your looking glass, Popsy," Erica said, holding it up. "No more pox. See?"

King Ken peered into the glass. His eyes lit up and he cried, *"I-yay ay-say!"*

The queen frowned. *"What,* Kenny?"

"I-yay ay-say ooray-hay!" cried the king. *"E-thay ox-pay ave-hay anished-vay!"*

The room grew suddenly still.

Wiglaf broke the silence. "The king just said, 'I say, hooray! The pox have vanished!' "

Now Daisy let out a squeal. "Gadzooks!"

she cried. "The king is speaking Pig Latin and I've got the pox!"

Wiglaf glanced at Daisy and gasped. From the tip of her snout to the ham of her hock, she was dotted with large, liver-colored spots.

Chapter 9

"Bats and blisters!" cried Zelnoc. "It's a switcheroo. Pox for the pig. Pig Latin for the king. I think I'll be going now."

"Not so fast, Wizard," said the queen. "How long will Kenny babble in this foreign tongue?"

"Beats me," said Zelnoc. "But look, Your Royal Highlyness, I got rid of his pox!"

"Now I've got 'em," said Daisy, scratching her snout with a front hoof.

"Oor-pay ig-pay!" said King Ken.

The queen buried her face in her hands. "Kenny is speaking gibberish!" she cried. "The pig has got the pox. There's no pheasant for the feast! Oh, woe is I!"

King Ken leaped out of his kingly bed.

"*Ig-pay!*" he cried. "*Ump-jay into-yay y-may ed-bay.*"

The king motioned for Daisy to jump into his bed.

Daisy stared at him in disbelief.

King Ken bent down and picked Daisy up.

"Kenny, no!" screamed Queen Barb.

The king plopped the pox-spotted pig down on his silken sheets.

"He's lost his mind!" shrieked the queen.

"Mumsy," said Erica. "Calm down."

"*Ere-thay!*" King Ken said happily. "*Ow-nay I'll-yay over-cay ou-yay up-yay!*" He pulled his velvet blanket up to Daisy's chin.

Daisy lowered her large pig's head onto King Ken's satin pillow. "Nice," she said.

"Wizard!" cried the queen. "Do something!"

"With pleasure, Your Highly Queenieness," said Zelnoc. "Stand back!"

The wizard began to twirl. Blue smoke swirled around his feet and rose until it covered him completely. When the smoke cleared, Zelnoc had vanished.

Queen Barb's crown slipped to the side of her head. "Fawnsley!" she cried. "Fawnsley!"

Fawnsley rushed into the room and bowed.

"Take me to the Royal Spa, Fawnsley," said the queen. "I need a relaxing soak in the hot tub!"

"Yes, Your Highness." Fawnsley bowed.

"*Y-bay y-bay, Arb-bay!*" said King Ken. He waved as Fawnsley led the queen away.

"My parents are so weird," muttered Erica.

"Don't worry," said Janice. "Everybody's are."

The queen was hardly gone when the door opened again. A small man wearing a puffy white cap stuck his head into the chamber.

"Hallo?" he called.

"Chef Pierre," said Erica. "Come in."

"Ef-chay Ierre-pay!" cried King Ken.

"Zut!" cried the chef, looking alarmed.

"My father is speaking a foreign language, Pierre," said Erica.

"Eet ees not French," said Pierre. "So! I come to tell you supper is—" He caught sight of Daisy propped up in the royal bed and his jaw dropped open. "A *cochon!*" he cried. "Een zee king's bed?"

"That is Daisy, Pierre," said Erica. "She's not feeling well."

"Day-zee!" Pierre exclaimed. He rushed over to the royal bed. "Oh, what a bee-u-ti-ful spotted peeg! Hallo, Day-zee!"

Daisy was too stunned to reply.

"Pardon me, Chef," said Angus. "But were you about to say supper is served?"

"Ah, *oui!*" said the chef. "In zee Blue Feasting Hall." He bowed to the king and left.

The king turned to Erica. *"Ell-way, Oppet-pay!"* he said. *"Et-lay us-yay all-yay ave-hay a-yay ice-nay upper-say."*

"Yes, let's have a nice supper," said Erica.

"Oming-cay, ig-pay?" asked the king.

"I think not, sire," said Daisy.

"Are you too ill to eat?" asked Wiglaf.

Daisy said, "I think I should stay here and rest a little longer."

Wiglaf thought she looked happy all snug in the king's giant bed.

"O-nay oblem-pray!" cried the king. *"Ou-yay all-shay ave-hay our-yay upper-say on-yay a-yay ay-tray."*

"My supper on a tray!" exclaimed Daisy. "Oh, thank you, Your Majesty. And...do you suppose a servant might bring me some books from the palace library?" she added. "I'm in the mood for a good mystery."

"O-nay oblem-pray!" said the king.

Daisy smiled and snuggled farther down

under the king's velvet blanket.

Wiglaf waited until the servant brought her a stack of books. Then he hurried down to the Blue Feasting Hall. The minstrel had said to stay close to Daisy. But surely there was no place safer for her than being tucked into the king's bed.

In the torch-lit feasting hall, King Ken sat at the head of a long table. Erica and Janice sat on his right. Wiglaf took a seat next to Angus on his left.

"*Eat-yay up-yay!*" the king said as servants began bringing in platters of food.

Wiglaf helped himself to Chef Pierre's roasted goose, boiled mutton, and yams.

"Yummers!" Angus cried. He licked mutton grease from his fingers. "Pass the yams, Wiglaf." He took several and gobbled them up. "Now for some goose!"

"*A-yay ood-gay eater-yay!*" said the king.

"Popsy?" said Erica. "Can you please stop

speaking Pig Latin?"

King Ken frowned. *"Et-lay e-may ee-say. Esting-tay! One-yay, wo-tay, ee-thray. Esting-tay!"* The king shook his head. *"O-nay, Oppet-pay. I-yay annot-cay op-stay."*

Erica sighed. "It's a good thing Daisy gave us Pig Latin lessons," she said. "At least we can understand you."

"Olly-jay ood-gay!" said the king.

The servant entered the dining room holding a freshly baked pie.

"Oh, joy!" cried Angus. "This must be Chef Pierre's famous cherry pie!"

"This is Chef Pierre's newest creation," said the servant. "A beezleberry pie."

"What?" cried Angus. "No, no! Say not so! For I am allergic to beezleberries!" He slumped down in his chair.

"What happens if you eat a beezleberry?" asked Wiglaf.

"Hives," said Angus. "One bite, and I'd have

twice as many spots as King Ken had before."

"*Ity-pay*," said the king. Then to the servant he said, "*Erve-say it-yay up-yay!*"

"Serve it up," Erica translated.

The servant cut the pie and handed Wiglaf a slice. He ate slowly, enjoying every delicious bite. He saved some for Daisy.

As the servant served the pie, Angus groaned, "This is the worst day of my life!"

"Hey! The minstrel was right, Angus!" exclaimed Janice suddenly. "You just said nay to pie! And hey—I met a wizard. My fortune came true, too."

Erica gasped. "And I saw spots!" she said. "All over you, Popsy!"

"*I-yay ay-say!*" said the king.

So the minstrel had not lost his fortune-telling powers after all, thought Wiglaf. Again, the minstrel's words came back to him: *Keep a close eye on your pig.*

A bad feeling crept over Wiglaf. Maybe it

had been unwise to leave Daisy alone. Perhaps he should go and check on her right now. He popped up from the table. But just then, the queen swept into the dining hall. Everyone rose and bowed, then sat back down. Wiglaf sat back down, too.

Queen Barb's crown was straight. She wore a fresh gown and oodles of jewels.

"Here I am, Kenny!" she said. "All refreshed. Had a lovely soak and an herbal wrap. Are you feeling better too, dear?"

"Olly-jay ood-gay!" said King Ken.

"Ohhhh," groaned the queen. "You're still speaking pig!"

"It-say own-day, Absie-bay," said King Ken. *"Ave-hay ome-say upper-say!"*

The queen turned pale. "Kenny," she said, "this pig talk has got to stop!"

The king shrugged. *"An't-cay op-stay."*

"He can't, Mumsy," said Erica. "He wants you to sit down and have some supper."

Queen Barb sank into her golden chair. "You've always babbled nonsense, Kenny. But at least before, I understood the words!" She pulled out her hankie and dabbed at her eyes. "Your subjects are coming to hear your speech. You've got to stop speaking pig by tomorrow!"

The servant set a golden plate in front of the queen. But she pushed it away.

"Remember what happened to that emperor who had no clothes, Kenny?" asked the queen. "Banished! If your subjects hear you talking pig, they'll rise up in arms. Oh, woe is us, Kenny! It will be the end of the kingdom!"

Chapter 10

aisy?" Wiglaf said softly as he cracked open the door to the king's chamber.

Everyone was still down in the feasting hall, except for Angus. Even without the pie, he had eaten way too much.

Now he was in one of the 435 bedrooms, lying down with a bellyache.

"Daisy?" Wiglaf called again. "I've brought your supper."

Daisy did not answer.

Wiglaf went in and put the supper tray on the bedside table. The bedcovers were rumpled. But the bed was empty.

"Daisy!" cried Wiglaf, looking around. "Where are you?"

Wiglaf searched the room. He raced up and down the torch-lit hallways, calling his pig. He opened door after door and called her name into the dark. But he found no sign of his pig. He lost his way for a while in the huge palace, but at last he found the Blue Feasting Hall. The king and queen had retired for the night.

"Daisy is missing!" cried Wiglaf. "We must find her!"

"This is the Royal Palace, Wiggie," said Erica. "What harm could come to her here?"

Her words made Wiglaf feel better. Yet he had to see his pig. He had to make sure she was all right.

"Let's all look for Daisy," Janice said.

"Daisy!" called Wiglaf as they peered into the Throne Room and Ballroom.

"Daisy girl!" he called as they looked in the Treasury and the Tapestry Room.

They asked every guard, servant, and lady-in-waiting they met along the way. But no one had seen Daisy.

At last they went to the Royal Kitchen. The palace cooks were busy making soup and baking pies and breads for tomorrow's feast.

"Has anyone seen a pig?" Erica asked.

"Not I, Princess," said the soup cook.

"Nor I," said the baker.

"Zee peeg?" said Chef Pierre. "*Oui*! I feex a *très bon* supper for zee peeg."

"You did?" cried Wiglaf. Relief flooded over him. "Then Daisy is all right!"

"*Oui*," said Pierre. "First, I send up zee supper. Zen I have zee servant take zee peeg to zee spa. She eez having a nice soak in zee hot toob right now."

Wiglaf smiled. Daisy in a hot tub! "She must like that."

The chef nodded. "And every hour I send her treats—pies and cakes and tarts. I take good care of zee peeg."

Hearing that, Wiglaf was content. And

very tired. Not long after that, Erica walked him to his room—a whole room all to himself. He climbed into a great big bed—big enough to hold him and his twelve beefy brothers without anybody falling out! He had a goose-down pillow. And a goose-down coverlet. To think, back in Pinwick, his bed had been a pile of straw!

Still, Wiglaf found it hard to sleep. For the queen paced up and down the hallway late into the night, sobbing loudly. King Ken yelled over the sobbing, trying to soothe her.

"On't-day orry-way, Absie-bay!" the king cried. *"I-yay ow-knay y-may eech-spay! Isten-lay!"* He cleared his throat. *"Adies-lay and-yay entlemen-gay! Easants-pay and-yay illagers-vay!"*

"We are doomed, Kenny!" wailed the queen. "Doomed!"

Wiglaf tried to think happy thoughts to help himself fall asleep. He imagined Daisy relaxing in the hot tub. He imagined giving

Molwena and Fergus the coin of Basilisk Gold. Fergus would bite it to make sure it was real gold. And Molwena would cry for joy. What was it that made this gold so special? Did each basilisk have twenty-four pieces of gold? If that was it, Basil now had only twenty-three coins. At last Wiglaf drifted off to sleep.

When he opened his eyes, the sun was shining brightly through the palace window. His tunic and leggings had been washed, pressed, and laid out for him. He was living like a prince! He threw on his clothes and hurried downstairs.

The royal family, Janice, and Angus were already sitting at the dining table.

"You slept through breakfast, Wiglaf," Angus said, seeming fully recovered. "And we've just finished lunch."

"Why don't *you* give the speech?" Erica was asking her sniveling, red-eyed mother.

"It has always been the king," said the

queen. "It *must* be the king! Oh, the kingdom is toast!"

"*I-yay ow-knay!*" cried the king. "*I-yay ill-way eclare-day Ig-pay Atin-lay e-thay official-yay anguage-lay of-yay e-thay ingdom-kay!*"

"What's that?" asked Queen Barb.

"The king said, 'I will declare Pig Latin the official language of the kingdom,' " Wiglaf told them.

"Our subjects can hardly speak English!" cried the queen. "They could never learn pig!" She began to weep again.

Now Chef Pierre entered the feasting hall.

He bowed and said, "*Bon!* Here eez zee menu for zee feast, your majesties. It does not matter zat we have no pheasant. I am preparing something else even better. It will be *magnifique!*" He handed Queen Barb a sheet of parchment.

Queen Barb dabbed at her nose with her

hankie as she read. "Fine," she said without enthusiasm. "If our subjects don't rebel. If there *is* a feast." She handed the menu to the king.

The king looked at it. *"Ery-vay ice-nay!"* he said, and he handed it to Erica.

"Let me see it!" said Angus eagerly.

Wiglaf looked on with Angus.

> *King Kenneth's Feast Day*
> *Water-Lily Soup*
> *Four and Twenty Blackbirds Baked in a Pie*
> *Braised Lucky Rabbits' Feet*
> *Grilled Pigeon Lips*
> *Herb-Marinated Cochon with Apple*
> *Chef Pierre's Surprise Pie*

Water-Lily Soup! Wiglaf had never heard of anything so exotic. But he did not like the idea of eating blackbirds. Or rabbits' feet. Or pigeon parts.

"What is '*cochon*'?" he asked Angus.

Angus shrugged. "I don't know, but it sounds delicious!"

Fawnsley stepped over to the boys and bowed. "I could not help but overhear your question," he said. "A *cochon* is a pig."

Wiglaf nodded. "Thank—" He stopped.

A *cochon* is a pig?

An herb-marinated *pig*?

Uh-oh!

Chapter II

aisy!" cried Wiglaf, leaping to his feet.

"Daisy what?" said Angus.

"Daisy is on the menu!" cried Wiglaf.

"I-yay ay-say!" cried the king.

"Where?" said Janice. "I don't see her."

"She is the *cochon!*" said Wiglaf. "Chef Pierre wants to cook her! Come on! We have to save Daisy!"

"Ohh!" wailed the queen as Erica jumped up with her friends. "What next?"

The four sped pell-mell up the marble stairs of the South Tower. They raced down the hallway to the Royal Spa. A blue-clad servant sat at the front desk.

"The pig!" cried Erica. "Where is she?"

"In the hot tub, last I looked, Princess," the servant said.

Off they raced to a steamy, sweet-smelling room. In its center was a great round tub.

Wiglaf stared at the steamy, swirling water. "Daisy's gone!" he cried. "Oh, this is all my fault! If only I had heeded the minstrel and kept watch on my pig!"

"And look!" said Angus. "A huge pile of empty plates!" He pointed to dirty dishes stacked beside the hot tub. "Chef Pierre has been fattening up Daisy!"

"To the kitchen!" shouted Janice.

Down the stairs they ran. They burst into the palace kitchen.

"Where is the pig?" Erica shouted to the bakers and roasters. "Tell us at once!"

"There she is!" cried Wiglaf. His eyes widened in horror, for Daisy was sitting up to her neck in steaming liquid inside a big, black cooking pot! A leafy bouquet was stuck into the cleft of one hoof. Her eyes were closed. Her skin had turned deep pink.

"We are too late!" cried Wiglaf. "She is cooked!" He ran to the tub and threw his arms around his pig.

Daisy's eyes fluttered open.

"She lives!" cried Angus.

"Oh, Daisy!" Wiglaf cried.

"Hello, Wiglaf," said Daisy dreamily. "I'm having an herbal soak. I sent a servant out to get blisterwort. I was just about to scatter these leaves in the tub to get rid of my pox. Oh, this bath feels heavenly." She gave a contented sigh.

"Quick!" cried Wiglaf. "We have to get her out of there!"

"Oh, no, please," said Daisy. "When else am I going to get such royal treatment? I want to enjoy it as long as I can!"

Wiglaf grabbed Daisy under one foreleg. Janice grabbed her under the other.

"One, two, three, heave!" called Janice.

They lifted the hot pink pig out of the pot. The leaves in Daisy's hoof went flying. Erica and Angus grabbed some dish towels and began drying her off.

"Why did you do that?" asked Daisy, near tears. "I love the hot tub!"

"That was no hot tub, Daisy," said Wiglaf. "That was a cooking pot!"

Daisy's eyes widened. "Noooo."

"I'm afraid he's right," said Erica.

"Look," said Angus. He held up the menu for the feast.

"*Cochon?*" Daisy's jaw dropped open. "You mean I've been *marinating?*"

Wiglaf and the others nodded.

Just then King Ken and Queen Barb rushed into the kitchen.

The cooks bowed.

"There you are, darling," the queen said to Erica. "I've been looking all over for you. We've decided to make a quick getaway. We must pack up—right now."

"What?" cried Erica.

"You mean there won't be any feast?" cried Angus.

The queen shook her head. "No speech, no feast," she said. "Come, darling. It's better this way. We'd best be gone when our subjects revolt."

"Excuse me, Your Royal Highnesses," said Daisy. "But I have read that wizards can work Undo Spells to reverse their own mistakes."

"Daisy!" said Wiglaf. "What are you saying?"

"I've always wanted to summon a wizard," Daisy went on. "When I spoke Pig Latin, that was impossible. But now I can do it! Ready? Conlez! Conlez! Conlez!"

A white flash lit the room and Zelnoc stood before them.

"*Ood-gay ief-gray!*" shrieked the king.

"Bats and bathtubs!" Zelnoc cried angrily.

He wore an apron over his star-bespeckled blue robe. "Am I summoned by a pig?"

"That's right," said Daisy.

"We're counting on you, dear Wizard!" said the queen.

"Ah, Your Highlyness!" Zelnoc bowed. Then he muttered, "This is what I get for leaving my summoner on—never a moment's peace! I just put a batch of Milky Way Shape-Shifters into the oven. Delightful pastries! One bite, and you take on any shape you wish. They'll be burned to a crisp by the time I get home again." He shot Daisy a dirty look. "So what'll it be, porker?"

"When last you were here, Zelnoc," Daisy said calmly, "your Get-Well Spell went wrong."

"Wrong?" said Zelnoc. "Not so. I was interrupted midspell. The accident turned the spell into a switcheroo. Pox for you. Pig Latin for the king."

"Whatever, Wizard," said Daisy. "The king

needs to speak proper English for his speech tonight. Have you got a spell to help him?"

"Please, Wizard, say yes," said the queen.

Zelnoc shrugged. "I can do an Undo Switcheroo Spell, but you won't like the results."

"What do you mean?" asked Janice.

"If I do an Undo Switcheroo, you'll be back where you started," Zelnoc explained. "A king with the pox."

"Oh, dear," said the queen.

"And you, porker," Zelnoc went on, "will be back to speaking Pig Latin."

All eyes turned to Daisy now.

She closed her eyes. "I do so enjoy expressing myself in proper English," she said with a great deal of feeling.

"*Up-yay o-tay ou-yay, Aisy-day,*" said the king.

"Make it snappy, pig," said Zelnoc. "You want the Undo Switcheroo or don't you? Tell me quick! I can smell my shape-shifters starting to burn around the edges."

Chapter 12

aisy heaved a great sigh and said, "If it weren't for your first Speech Spell, Zelnoc, I'd never have spoken at all. And speaking Pig Latin is better than oinking."

"Then you'll let Zelnoc do the Undo Switcheroo, Daisy?" asked Erica.

"Yes." Daisy nodded. "For the good of the kingdom. And don't worry about King Ken's pox. I can get rid of them."

"Oh, thank you, Daisy!" cried the queen. "You are a fine swine indeed!"

"Ready-o?" said Zelnoc. He plucked his wand from where he'd parked it behind his left ear. "Pig, you stand by the window," he said. "King? You by the chopping block."

Daisy walked slowly toward her spot.

The king took his place as well.

"Everyone else, stand back," said the wizard. "And don't interrupt!"

Zelnoc waved his wand in a great circle and began to chant:

> *Hickety, pickety*
> *The spell is undone*
> *By counting backward*
> *Three, two, one!*

Zelnoc waved his wand over King Ken and shouted, *"Three!"*

Then the wizard waved his wand over Daisy and shouted, *"Two!"*

Next, he touched his wand to his own forehead and he kicked up his heels, dancing a silly little jig. As he swept his wand in a big circle, Pierre rushed into the kitchen.

"One!" shouted the wizard.

"I say!" shouted the king.

"Ah! Zere is zee *cochon*!" cried the chef. He ran for Daisy, "Come, peeg! I weel roast you now!"

"Elp-hay!" cried Daisy.

"Keep away from her, Pierre!" cried King Ken. "This pig is about to save my royal hide."

Chef Pierre skidded to a halt. "Zee peeg?"

The king nodded. "Say one more word about roasting Daisy, and you're fired!"

"Oh, deed I say roast her?" cried Pierre. "No, no, no. I mean to say toast her! *Oui!* Tonight we weel dreenk a toast to this beautiful peenk peeg!"

"That's more like it," said King Ken.

"Anks-thay, Ing-kay En-kay," said Daisy.

"My Undo Switcheroo worked like a charm," said Zelnoc. "Now, back to my baking." With a flash of light, he vanished.

"I'd forgotten how much these pox itch!"

wailed the king as he started scratching himself again.

"*Iglaf-way? Elp-hay e-may,*" Daisy asked.

Wiglaf followed Daisy as she trotted over to the pot. She motioned for him to pick up the leaves scattered around it.

"*Isterwort-blay eaves-lay,*" she said.

She instructed Wiglaf to place the blisterwort leaves on the king's skin. He did so. When he peeled them off, the pox had vanished.

"Oh!" cried the queen. "Daisy, you have saved the kingdom. We must give you a royal thank-you. Would you like a medal with King Ken's picture on it, dear?"

"*I-yay uess-gay,*" said Daisy.

"Or we could declare you Lady Daisy," said the queen.

"*Ine-fay,*" Daisy said quietly.

"Hmm," said the queen. "How about coming back to the palace once a year for a day at the Royal Spa?"

Daisy smiled. *"Es-yay, Our-yay Ajesty-may!"* she said. Then she looked at Pierre and added, *"O-nay icks-tray!"*

"No tricks," Wiglaf translated.

"Nevair!" Chef Pierre bowed to the king and queen. "Instead of *cochon*, I weel make a vegetable stew fit for a king and queen."

"Perfect, Pierre," said the queen. She gasped. "Listen! Do you hear that?"

Outside the palace, Wiglaf heard people laughing and shouting, "Speech! Speech! Come on, King Ken! We're waiting."

"Our subjects are here!" cried the queen. "Oh, Kenny. I know you're going to give the very best speech ever! Come. We must get you into your royal-blue velvet robe."

For Wiglaf, the next few hours sped by in a happy whirl of excitement. He and his friends joined the subjects in the courtyard for King Ken's speech. He forgot almost all of it except for the last line about ordering up a walloping big feast. Since this was all his subjects wanted to hear anyway, they cheered and shouted, "Long live King Ken!"

Now Wiglaf knew there would be no more talk of drafting Bob of Bobbinshire to be king.

After the speech, everyone sat down at long tables on the palace lawn. Servants brought in Chef Pierre's feast. Wiglaf thought he had never tasted anything so fine as his vegetable stew.

Janice said, "It will be hard to go back to DSA tomorrow."

"Back to Frypot's cooking!" cried Angus. He swiped his bread around his bowl to get every last bit of stew.

Wiglaf did the same. "I wonder how the Alchemy Convention went," he said. "Maybe Mordred finally has enough gold."

"Nah," said Angus. "Uncle Mordred's moneymaking schemes always backfire. They're as bad as Zelnoc's spells."

Wiglaf smiled. Angus was right. And that meant that Headmaster Mordred would be all the more amazed when Wiglaf showed him his Basilisk Gold. He reached into his pocket to touch his treasure. But...his pocket was empty.

"My Basilisk Gold!" he cried. "It is gone!"

"Do you have a hole in your pocket?" asked Janice.

Wiglaf shook his head.

"Did you put it away for safekeeping?" asked Erica.

"No," Wiglaf said.

"Did you spend it?" asked Angus.

"No!" cried Wiglaf. "But I should have." He hit himself on the forehead. "Now I remember what is so special about Basilisk Gold—you must spend it within twenty-four hours or it disappears."

Wiglaf was sad to lose his golden treasure. But here he was, a lowly peasant from Pinwick, feasting at the Royal Palace. And here came a servant carrying a huge tray of pies and cakes and tarts. And who knew what wondrous surprises the journey back to DSA might bring?

How to Speak Pig Latin

King Ken

I say, speaking Pig Latin is jolly good fun.
My jester and I speak it anytime we don't want
Queen Barb to know what we're saying! And
Pig Latin is so easy—if I can speak it, anyone
can! *Ave-hay un-fay!*

If a word begins with a consonant, move the first letter to the end of the word and add "-ay."

Wiglaf = Iglaf-way

palace = alace-pay

gold = old-gay

If a word begins with two or more consonants, move them to the end of the word and add "-ay."

dragon = agon-dray

slayer = ayer-slay

scram = am-scray

If a word begins with a vowel, add "-yay" to the end of the word.

Angus = Angus-yay

academy = academy-yay

eel = eel-yay